DETROIT PUBLIC LIBRARY
3 5674 00750797 4

W9-CKJ-033

DATE DUE

THEODORE ALL GROWN UP

THEODORE ALL GROWN UP

by Ellen Stoll Walsh

Doubleday & Company, Inc., Garden City, New York

Library of Congress Cataloging in Publication Data

Walsh, Ellen Stoll.
Theodore all grown up.

SUMMARY: Theodore considers himself quite grown up until he starts giving away his toys.
I. Title.
PZ7.W1675Th [E]
Library of Congress Catalog Number 80-2244
ISBN: 0-385-15868-8 Trade
ISBN: 0-385-15869-6 Prebound

Printed in the United States of America
First Edition

For David, who likes books with pictures

Theodore woke up one morning and stretched his legs. He stretched them as far as he could until "thump," his feet hit the foot of his bed. He stretched his arms as far as he could and "bump," his hands hit the head of his bed.

He picked up his little cloth piglet. "Look, Stuffy, I'm as big as my bed," he said. "I must have grown up in the night!"

Theodore had always wanted to be grown up. He thought of all the wonderful things grown-ups do. "Now I'll be able to stay up all night if I want to," he told Stuffy.

"And I'll lie in bed and read those fat books that don't have pictures. I'll even be able to warm up my bath by myself when the water starts to get cold."

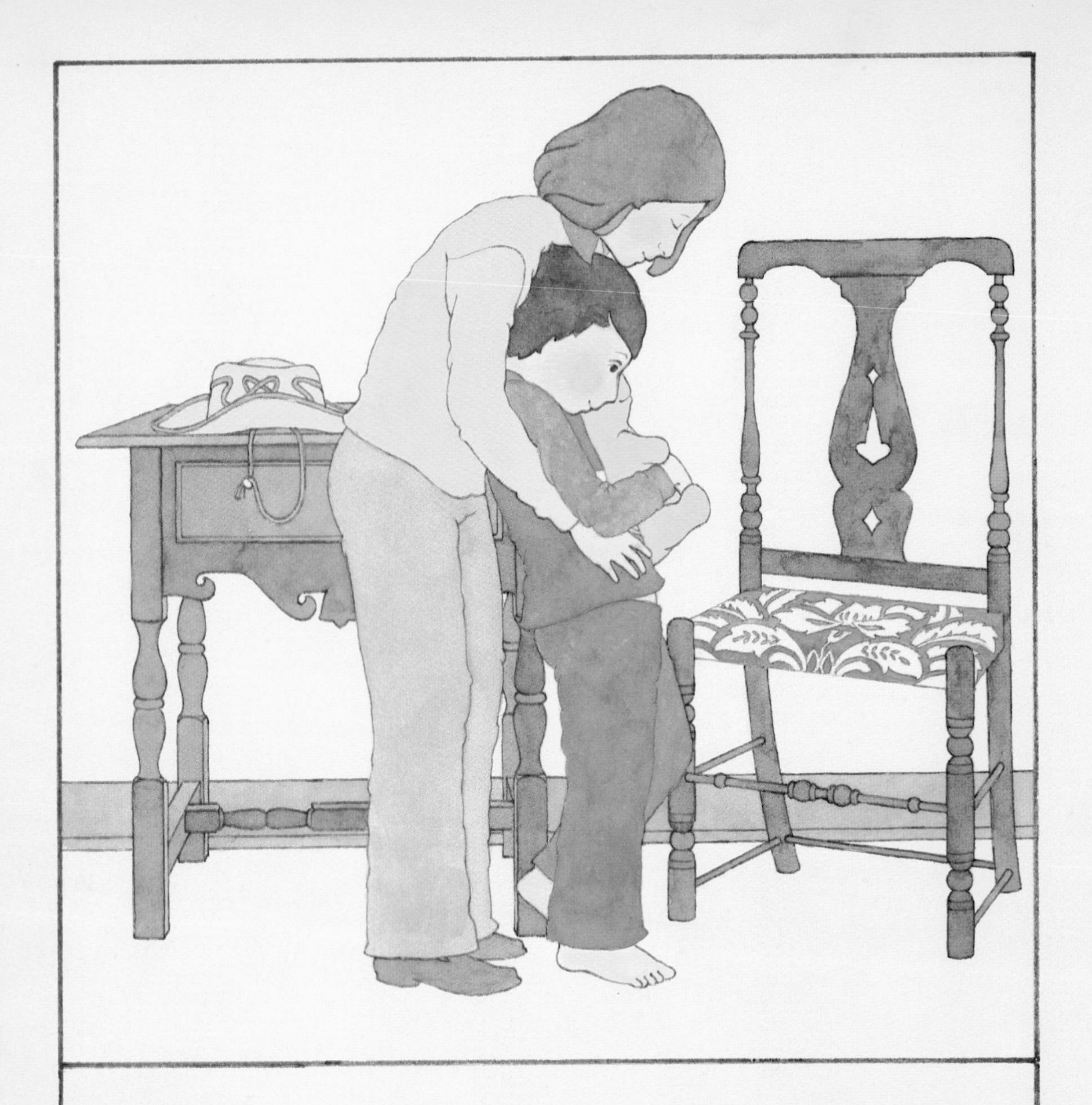

Theodore was very excited. He went to tell his mother. "You still look like my little boy to me," she said, and she gave him a hug. "But if you have really grown up, you will probably want to give Stuffy to some nice little boy."

"Oh,"said Theodore, "that might upset Stuffy too much. I'll just put him on my bookcase for now and pretend he is a statue."

Then Theodore went to tell his father. "You still look like my little boy to me," said his father, and he gave him a tickle. "But if you are sure you are a grown-up, you must decide what to do with your toys."

"I guess I had better give them away," said Theodore. "I will just run and check through them to make sure there are no grown-up things mixed in."

Theodore pulled an airplane out of his toy box. "Grown-ups don't play with toy airplanes," he said, and he started a give-away pile.

Theodore put his Indian drum and his wooden elephant with the airplane.

He started to put his ball in the give-away pile. Then he remembered. “Sometimes grown-ups play ball with little kids,” he said, and he rolled it safely out of the way.

A few toys that had been broken for a long time were easy to give away, but Theodore was sad to give up his spaceships. He zoomed around the room with them one last time before putting them down carefully in the give-away pile.

The give-away pile grew bigger and bigger. The ball looked very lonely all by itself.

Theodore looked at Stuffy. Even Stuffy was tired of being a statue. He was asleep in the cowboy hat. Theodore sighed. Perhaps being a grown-up would be harder than he had thought.

"Oh," said Theodore happily, "I forgot. Grown-up Indians play Indian drums." He took the drum from the give-away pile and sang a little Indian song before putting it with his ball. He felt a little better.

Theodore kept looking at his give-away pile. He could not help thinking about his spaceships. "The kid who gets my spaceships will be lucky," he thought. "They have lights and buzzers and lots of little men inside."

"Uh oh," said Theodore, "what if he doesn't like spaceships? Or maybe he is just careless with his toys. Then he might break them and lose the little men. I think I had better keep them, at least for now!"

Theodore buzzed the buzzers and flashed the lights as he landed his spaceships safely next to his ball.

Theodore took his sailboat out of his toy box. "Maybe the kid who will get my toys doesn't like sailboats either," he said hopefully. "But I guess any kid would have to like this one. It has cloth sails and rigging that really works."

"But what if he gets his fingers pinched by the rudder? He might get upset and never play with it again. Then it would be wasted. Maybe I should keep it too. Just for now." And he sailed it over next to his spaceships.

The last thing in Theodore's toy box was his super cape. It was just like the cape that Wonder Boy wore in the movie. When Theodore ran with his cape flapping in the wind behind him, he felt like he was really flying.

He held it up. “This cape is too big for a little kid,” he said. “He could be blown away by the wind. The kid who gets this cape should be at least as big as I am.”

Theodore thought for a minute. "And if he has to be at least as big as I am," he said, "then he might as well be me!"

Theodore snapped on his super cape, grabbed Stuffy, and ran to tell his mother and father.

"I guess I am still your little boy," he said, and they were glad.

When Theodore went back to his toys, he went through them very carefully. He put a few toys that he had really outgrown into a new give-away pile. He put the rest back into his toy box. "I guess I have grown up a bit after all," he said.

All day Theodore and Stuffy played and pretended and did wonderful tricks. Theodore was the same happy boy he had been yesterday, and would most certainly be tomorrow. He was glad. And Stuffy was, too!